ALISON ON THE TRAIL
by Catherine Connor

Illustrations by
Gabriel Picart

Spot Illustrations by
Rich Grote

MAGIC ATTIC PRESS

Published by Magic Attic Press.

For more information contact:
Book Editor, Magic Attic Press, 866 Spring Street,
P.O. Box 9722, Portland, ME 04104-5022.

First Edition
Printed in the United States of America
1 2 3 4 5 6 7 8 9 10

Betsy Gould, Editorial Director
Marva Martin, Art Director
Robin Haywood, Managing Editor

Edited by Judit Bodnar
Designed by Susi Oberhelman

ISBN 1-57513-010-6

Magic Attic Club books are printed on acid-free, recycled paper.

As members of the
MAGIC ATTIC CLUB,
we promise to
be best friends,
share all of our adventures in the attic,
use our imaginations,
have lots of fun together,
and remember—the real magic is in us.

Alison   Keisha

Heather   Megan

Table of Contents

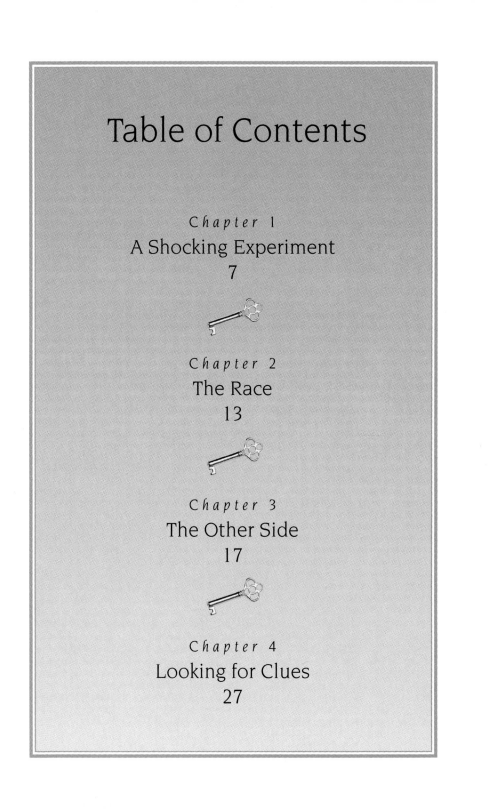

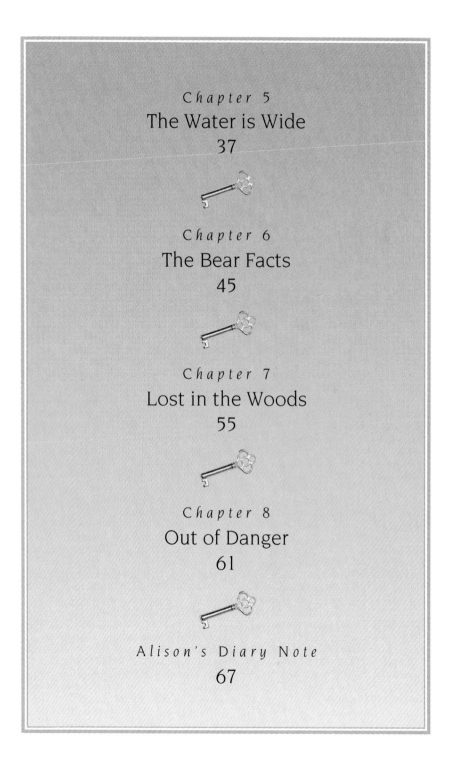

Chapter

One

A SHOCKING EXPERIMENT

can't believe Science is my favorite class this year,"
said Heather Hardin, shaking her head. "I never used
to like it," she added.

"We never had Ms. Joseph before," said Alison McCann,
adjusting the blue backpack on her shoulder as she walked
to school with her friends. "She's the coolest teacher we've
ever had. She could make a drink of water seem interesting."

Keisha Vance laughed. "Actually, a drink of water *can be*
interesting. Remember when we put the drop of pond water

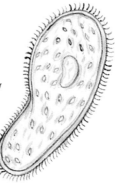

on the slide and looked at it under the microscope? I *loved* watching that paramecium do its thing! First, there's only one. And then before you know it, the cell divides and there are two!"

"Wouldn't it be cool if we could do that in real life?" Megan Ryder said. "If there were two of me, I could live here with Mom and Aunt Frances, and travel with Dad when he's on assignment . . . all at the same time."

The four best friends picked up their pace as they neared Lincoln School. Every morning they met at the corner and went to school together. Mostly they just talked, but every once in a while they practiced for a test while they walked, especially if they had one of Ms. Austin's monthly spelling tests. "Comprehensives," the teacher called the tests that she gave the last Friday of every month. The girls always studied hard for them. Alison worked hardest of all, and was already preparing for the one scheduled for the end of this week.

"I wish spelling were as easy for me as it is for you," Alison said to Megan wistfully.

"It's not exactly *easy* for me," Megan said. "It's just that I know if I'm going to be a travel writer, I have to know how to spell."

Alison tapped Megan on the arm. "Not anymore," she said, "thanks to the miracle of the spell checker on the computer." She paused a moment, thinking of how hard she struggled with spelling. No matter what people said or how teachers taught her, she just couldn't remember how to spell certain words.

"Too bad miracles couldn't help us on Ms. Austin's last comprehensive," said Keisha.

"Give us a break," said Heather. "You made an A."

"But I missed two out of fifty," said Keisha, who knew she had to make good grades if she was going to become a veterinarian.

Alison laughed and rolled her eyes. "If I did that well on one of Ms. Austin's comprehensives, I'd send an announcement to the *Herald*!"

"And so," said Ms. Joseph to her science students later that day, "just as a magnetic field can produce electricity in a wire, a dry cell battery can, too. Think of electricity as water running through a hose," she said, demonstrating her words at the lab faucet in the front of the room. "Amperage is the amount of electricity produced. The bigger the hose, the more electricity you generate. Voltage is the pressure of the water flowing through the hose. The harder you turn on the water," she turned the faucet on full force and held tight to the small hose so it wouldn't spray all over the room, "the more power or voltage you get."

Alison nodded as she hastily scribbled notes in her science notebook, eager to get on with that day's lab experiment.

"Okay," Ms. Joseph continued, "let's break up into groups of threes or fours and choose a table so you can do your own experiments."

The four best friends glanced at each other and nodded. They didn't need to speak. Each knew what the other was thinking. Alison and Megan and Keisha had been friends for years, and Heather had recently joined the tight-knit group. Their friendship had been cemented when they formed the Magic Attic Club.

Ellie Goodwin, an older woman in the neighborhood, had invited the girls to explore her attic, where they found an antique trunk full of wonderful outfits. The girls discovered that if they put on an outfit and stood in front of her old-fashioned mirror, they would be transported on an adventure. That secret had transformed their friendship into something more special than ever . . . something that Alison and the girls treasured.

"Today," said the science teacher, once the class had settled in their groups, "we're going to connect a light using a motorcycle battery, coated copper wires and an automobile brake bulb."

"Cool," whispered Alison, looking at the bulb that rested in a porcelain stand.

"Keep in mind what I said about Benjamin Franklin," Ms. Joseph continued. "He was lucky he didn't get electrocuted when he flew that kite in the storm to prove that lightning was electricity. Electricity can be a lifesaver or a killer, depending on how you treat it. And it must always be treated with care and respect. Do you understand?"

All the kids nodded.

"Before we start," said Ms. Joseph, "there are some safety rules that you *must* remember. If you don't observe these rules, someone could get hurt." She paused, making certain every student in the room was paying attention. "Once the wires are attached to the battery, never touch the uncovered copper ends together. The covering on the wire protects you. If you touch the *exposed* wires, your body will complete the electrical circuit and you could get a shock. Now, is everything clear? Does anyone have any questions?"

Nobody raised a hand. "Then let's get to work." Ms. Joseph removed the rubber coating from the ends of her copper wires with a wire stripper.

As Keisha carefully stripped each wire for her table, Alison heard someone go "Psst!" Then she felt a tap on her shoulder. When she turned around, Ben Benchley was leaning in her direction.

"Want to see whose table gets the light turned on first?" challenged Ben. "I'll bet we can beat you."

Alison glanced at Ben's table. Noah Cummings, Linda Chang, and Rachel Harmon looked at her expectantly.

Alison grinned and her blue eyes lit up. "You're on!"

Chapter

Two

THE
RACE

lison loved competition. She was an excellent athlete, and her competitive spirit often carried over into other areas of her life. Whether it was a soccer match or a science experiment, she enjoyed making a game out of what she was doing. She also liked to win and she was eager to be the first to light the bulb. Alison waited impatiently as Heather carefully wound the copper ends of the two wires around the screws on the battery.

"Now screw down the wires so they're tightly connected,"

Alison told Keisha. "But hurry!" she whispered, glancing around. "Ben's table is ahead of us!"

"Come on, Ali," said Keisha. "You're president of the class, not president of the science table. Besides," she added, "*we* didn't make the bet. *You* did."

Alison shrugged. "C'mon. A game can make projects like this more fun," she said. "I thought you'd like it."

"We do," said Megan. "But we still have to be careful."

"I know, I know. . . . But being careful doesn't mean we can't be fast," Alison said. "Are you ready yet?"

"Hang on a minute," Megan said, positioning the porcelain base so she could insert the wires.

Turning in her chair, Alison checked out the progress at Ben's table. "Hurry!" she said.

Megan reached out her hand. "Okay, I'm ready."

Alison glanced at the table next to her as she shoved the wires at Megan. A blue spark arced from one wire to another.

"Ow!" cried Megan. She jumped, and the porcelain bulb holder crashed to the floor.

Suddenly, Ms. Joseph was standing at the table inspecting Megan's finger. "It was just a little shock, Megan," she said. "Nothing to worry about. Running some cold water on your finger will help."

Megan nodded, gingerly rubbing her finger. A faint

redness marked the place Alison had touched with the exposed wires.

Ms. Joseph put her hand on Megan's shoulder as she looked around the table. "First thing, though, I want to know how this happened."

"Well," said Keisha. "We were trying to hurry because . . . because . . ." She glanced at Alison.

"We had the wires connected to the battery," said Heather. "Then . . . then Alison took the wires—"

"It was my fault," said Alison, hating to look her

favorite teacher in the eyes.

Ms. Joseph frowned in dismay. "You, Alison?" She paused a moment. "I'm surprised."

"Yes," she said in a barely audible voice. Alison could feel every kid in the class staring at her as her cheeks began to redden.

"I thought my instructions were quite simple and clear. Weren't you listening, Alison?"

"Yes, but we were . . . I was in a hurry because . . . because I wanted us to be the first table to light up the bulb," she said, staring hard at the surface of the table. She wanted to crawl in a hole and disappear.

"I'm disappointed." Ms. Joseph was solemn and stern. "I didn't expect carelessness from you."

Alison blinked, resenting the way that Ms. Joseph was talking to her in front of the whole class. "I'm sorry," she mumbled, scuffing her sneakers nervously.

The teacher nodded. "Who are you apologizing to?"

"To you." Alison's eyes never left the table.

"And?" Ms. Joseph asked quietly, guiding her answer.

"And," said Alison, glancing quickly at her friends, "to Heather and Keisha and Megan . . . especially Megan."

"That's okay," Megan whispered.

chapter Three

THE
OTHER
SIDE

ren't you coming with us?" Heather asked Alison.
"I can't," Alison said to Heather, Megan, and
Keisha after school. "I have to stop by the market and
pick up a couple of things for my mom."

Heather looked at Alison. "Are you sure?" she asked.

Alison nodded, hoping they believed her.

"Well . . ." said Keisha, "I guess we better get going."

"Okay," Alison mumbled.

"So we'll see you in the morning?" Heather asked.

"Right," said Alison.

Watching her three friends stroll down the sidewalk together, Alison was tempted to run after them. She felt frustrated and left out. At the same time, she was angry with her favorite teacher for embarrassing her in front of the whole class. It isn't fair. I'm not the only one to blame, she thought. If Megan had been paying attention, she would have taken the insulated section of the wires. Besides, no one really got hurt, so why did Ms. Joseph have to make such a big deal out of it?

Alison waited until her friends were out of sight and then started on a different route home. By the time she'd walked a block, she had decided to stop by Ellie's attic.

Maybe a new adventure in Ellie's attic will take my mind off what happened at school, she thought.

Alison unlocked the door with the scrolled golden key and turned on the light. She hurried up the steps into the attic, eager to find something really different. Looking around the room, she walked over to the huge mahogany wardrobe and picked up a wide-brimmed hat trimmed with plumes. Shaking her head, she

replaced the hat and wandered over to the small antique writing desk. Then she opened the lid and looked inside.

A small photo album caught her eye. It was filled with pictures of the various places around the world where Ellie Goodwin had traveled. In one photo the Eiffel Tower stood in its famous Parisian setting. In another picture was Buckingham Palace, and another of Big Ben with its clock and towers.

Alison placed the album on the desk and walked over to the old-fashioned steamer trunk. As she opened the heavy top and looked inside, she thought, what's it going to be today? What would be really special? London? Montana? The South Seas?

Rummaging through the trunk, she checked out a riding outfit. Not in the mood for horses today, she thought. Then she reached deep inside and pulled out a drawstring bag. In it were a variety of items: hiking boots, a backpack, and a hiking outfit.

She slipped quickly into the navy-and-white striped shirt, matching navy shorts, and red jacket. Without hesitating, she reached for the hiking boots, sat on the floor, and put them on. Then she stood up and looked at her reflection in the mirror.

Make this a good one, she wished. Make this an extra special trip.

She didn't feel any movement, anything different at all. The only thing she noticed was the smell. At first she couldn't identify it. Then it began to remind her of Christmas trees.

Alison looked around. She was standing near a rushing stream in a valley surrounded by pine-covered mountains. Spruces and cedars grew in haphazard clusters all around her. At her feet, pine cones decorated the leaf-covered ground.

Where am I? she thought, suddenly afraid she was lost in the wilderness.

Then she heard a voice calling her.

"Alison? Aren't you Alison?"

She turned to see a girl running toward her. "Yes."

"We're almost ready!" said the girl.

Alison smiled nervously. What do I do now?

The girl stopped right in front of her. She appeared to be about seven years old. "Are you coming?" she asked.

Alison nodded. "Sure," she said, trying to figure out what was happening as she adjusted her backpack. "I'll . . . I'll be right with you."

Not far ahead, at the edge of the valley, was a large stone-and-log building. To one side of the building, seven small log cabins peeked out from thick clusters of pines.

In front of the larger building, a broad green playing field was marked for soccer. Beyond one end of the field, a volleyball net wafted in the breeze; at the other, a large open-sided tent was set up. A faint path disappeared in the dark piney green of the mountain slope.

Alison followed the girl to a cabin. In the doorway, three girls stood waiting beneath a carved wooden sign that read "Sierra."

As Alison approached, a slender, athletic young woman peered around the girls and stepped outside. She smiled warmly as she extended her hand in greeting.

"Welcome to Camp Vista, Alison. I'm Becky Wong, the Senior Counselor for Sierra cabin. Thanks so much for filling in at the last minute. When Kelly got sick and had to go home, I didn't know what I'd do. I have several other cabins to supervise, too."

"I'm happy to help out," Alison said, shaking Becky's suntanned hand.

"I see you've already met Kate." She cocked her head toward the tall, gangly girl beside Alison.

"Yes." Alison nodded and smiled at Kate.

"As Sierra cabin's Junior Counselor, you'll be in charge of Kate and her cabinmates. This is Jackie . . . and Kimberly . . . and Anna." Becky touched each girl's shoulder in turn. "Girls, bring out your gear while I fill

Alison in on this afternoon's schedule."

The four campers eagerly scurried in and out of the cabin while Becky briefed Alison about them and explained what she was to do. She carefully pointed out the hiking path on Alison's map and showed her the most important landmarks.

Then she asked Alison to be sure and remind the girls always to stay on the trail and never lose sight of each other and of her. "Once they're ready," she said, "the hike itself should take a couple of hours. That will get you to the overnight site around five o'clock, in plenty of time for a swim and to get a campfire going for the cookout."

"And one last thing," Becky added. "Remind the girls not to pick or eat any wild berries, no matter how good they look." Then she left the new Junior Counselor to get to know her group and help them prepare their packs.

"Okay," said Alison a short time later as she went over the checklist one last time. "Are your water bottles filled?"

"Mine's right here," said Jackie. Her ponytail, secured high on her head, bounced when she talked.

"Yes!" said the other girls.

"Do you have your snacks?" Alison tried to make her voice sound official but not bossy.

Kate held up her backpack. "We sure do!" she said.

"Kimberly?" Becky had told Alison that this dark-eyed camper was a little shy and needed to be drawn out.

"I have all my stuff, too," Kimberly said.

"What about extra socks?"

Anna nodded vigorously, the copper curls that framed her freckled face bobbing with every move of her head.

"Did everybody remember to pack a jacket, bug spray, and sunscreen?"

The girls could hardly stand still. "Yes! Yes! Yes!" they cried. "Can we go now?"

Alison laughed, delighted by their enthusiasm. The mood was contagious. Besides, she wasn't used to being in charge of kids who looked up to her with such excitement and expectation. Alison felt terrific.

"We're a little late getting started, but there's one more thing I have to tell you," she said. "I guess you know the other counselors have gone on ahead. We're supposed to meet the other hiking groups at the tent site before suppertime. Did you know there's also something extra special about the hike today?"

"Ooh, what is it?" Jackie asked.

"Weeell . . ." Alison said slowly. "We're supposed to

follow a trail that's been marked especially for us. We'll have to be very alert and look for clues—broken branches and secret arrows, things that point out the way we're supposed to go." Although the counselors had marked the trail so the campers could have fun looking for markers, Alison felt in her pocket to make certain her trail map was there.

"Cool!" cried Jackie and Kate. Anna tossed her hat in the air, and Kimberly's face broke into a broad smile.

"Then let's be off!" Alison's grin was as eager as Kimberly's.

Chapter

Four

LOOKING
FOR CLUES

hat's the most important rule?" Alison asked as they headed out.

"We stay together and we look out for each other," the campers chorused.

Single file, they started up the path that wound uphill behind the log cabins. In no time, the camp and the lodge were out of sight, hidden by the lush foliage of the trees. The trail was padded with thick layers of damp leaves and evergreen needles, and Alison felt as if she

were walking on sponges. Glancing behind her, she counted heads, then said, "Okay kids, the secret to climbing uphill without getting overly tired is to keep a slow steady pace. Pretty soon the trail will level out. Then we'll walk a little faster so we can get to the campground by sundown."

"Maybe if we hurry, we can be the first ones there," said Kate.

Anna looked at Kate. "We don't need to be the first ones there."

"Yes we do," said Kate. "There's a secret prize for the group that gets to the tent site first."

Alison smiled. "Becky didn't mention that. Are you sure?"

Kate shrugged. "It's what I heard. A girl named Janet Higgens in Teton cabin said that the group that gets there last makes up the beds the next day for the group that gets there first."

"That's great!" said Anna. "Making beds is such a drag! We better get going!"

Alison stopped. "Wait a minute!" she said. "First of all, I haven't heard anything about a contest. Second of all, if there *is* such a contest, it wouldn't be fair to have it unless we knew about it in advance. And last of all, if we hurry too fast we might miss some of the clues along the way. So I'm putting my money on this secret prize being just a rumor."

"Well," said Kate, "the prize might be a rumor, but I still want to get to the tent site before Janet's cabin. They always think they can do things better than anybody else."

"What is it, Kimberly?" Alison asked.

"Can't we even *try* to hurry? You could get your bed made up, too," said Kimberly shyly.

"We'll see, Kimberly." she said.

Alison turned to the girls. "Does anybody see anything unusual?" she asked. The girls looked in every direction. "Pay attention, now. We're looking for trail clues, remember?"

"There!" said Anna, pointing to an arrow formed out of small stones that had been laid next to the path.

"You got it!" said Alison, giving Anna a pat on the back. "So what does that mean, Kate?"

"We take the right fork?"

"Right!"

At first the girls chattered as they walked along, but the sights and sounds of the forest soon hushed them and slowed their pace. Squirrels scampered in the trees above hoping to find some nuts. Mountain chickadees searched for bugs hiding in the branches and ravens flew overhead.

"Hear that hammering sound?" Alison whispered.

The girls nodded.

"It's a woodpecker. Look way up in the tree and you can see his little red head moving back and forth."

Jackie swung her head, flipping her ponytail dramatically. "How do you know it's a him?" she asked.

"Because of his bright coloring." As Alison spoke, the sound of distant thunder rumbled through the mountains. Gray clouds were forming on the northern horizon.

Kimberly looked up at the sky and shivered. "I hate thunderstorms," she said. "My uncle Nathan got struck by lightning when he was ten years old."

Alison put her hand on Kimberly's shoulder. "The thunder was nowhere near us. We don't have anything to worry about," she said. "So come on now. . . . Let's stop talking so much and move along, or we'll never reach the campground before dinner. We still have to find the stream and then hike another two miles or so."

"I'm thirsty!" Kate complained.

Alison laughed. "That's why you carry a water bottle."

The group stopped briefly to rest and have a drink. When Alison glanced at her watch and then at the sky, a chill went through her. The clouds were rolling in more quickly than she had figured. The last thing she wanted was to get caught in a storm . . . or worse, be out here with the girls after dark.

"I'll tell you what," Alison said. "It's almost four o'clock now. The weather seems to be getting cooler, so why don't we all put on our jackets? Now, what do you say we do some serious hiking for thirty or forty minutes. We can sit down for a *real* rest after that." She paused, then asked. "Is that a deal?"

With just a little bit of grumbling, the girls agreed.

They started out at a lively pace, but they hadn't walked more than a hundred yards or so when they came to another fork in the trail. The group halted.

This left fork must be the shortcut I saw on the map, thought Alison, but Becky said to stick to the marked trail.

"Which way do we go?" asked Kate, looking at the two paths.

"What do you think?" Alison asked.

"Maybe we should follow the broken branches on the bush there and go that way," said Kimberly, pointing to the right fork.

Alison smiled. "Good job!" she said. "I might have missed that clue if you hadn't pointed it out."

A flash of lightning lit the sky.

Alison counted off the seconds between the lightning

and the clap of thunder that followed. Twenty seconds. Uh-oh. The storm is only a few miles away.

She looked at the girls for their reaction. Fear filled Kimberly's dark eyes.

"Wow! That thunder is *loud*! But it doesn't mean it's going to hurt you. I promise you there's nothing to worry about. If we hurry, we'll all be safe in our tents before the first drop of rain falls on the ground."

Anna shook her head uncertainly. "But I counted the time between the lightning and the thunder," she said. "The storm isn't very far away."

"I know," said Alison. "But storms can travel in lots of directions or they can get stalled along the way. So let's not worry."

"What will we do if it *does* get here?" Jackie asked.

Once again lightning flashed in the sky. An ominous, low rumble followed.

"Listen, kids," said Alison, looking at the fork in the trail. "We'll just take the left that I saw marked on the map. That will get us to the tent site sooner than we thought." Alison reached into her pocket for the map. Oh no! Both of her pockets were totally empty. She must have lost the map during the last rest stop.

"Would you show us the shortcut on the map?" Anna asked sweetly.

Alison smiled. "Trust me on this one," she said. "We don't want to waste any time right now. So let's save the map reading until later and get hiking."

"Kimberly, you found the last clue, so why don't you take the lead for awhile." Alison nodded to the shortcut on the left.

In spite of her fear, Kimberly beamed proudly as she stepped ahead of her leader and motioned for everyone to follow her down the shortcut. Now that the trail had leveled out, Alison encouraged Kimberly to keep up a lively pace.

Suddenly Kimberly put up her hand. Behind her, Alison and the three other campers came to a halt. "Hear that?" Kimberly said.

Everyone stood perfectly still. In the distance they heard a whooshing, rolling sound.

"It's the storm!" said Jackie.

"No," said Kimberly. "It must be the stream we're supposed to cross. We're almost there."

"My foot hurts," said Kate. "I think I have a blister."

Alison sighed. Figuring that a snack might give them extra energy, she decided to make a brief stop. "Right after our snack, we'll cross the stream and go straight on to the campsite without stopping. It's only a mile or so from there. Is that okay?"

The girls nodded.

The group moved to the clearing, sat down, and unwrapped their sandwiches, apples, and granola bars. Alison was surprised at how hungry she was. As soon as they finished, everybody but Jackie put the wrappers in their backpacks. She dropped hers on the ground.

Alison glanced at the wrapper.

"Do you all remember the hiking rule about the food and containers we bring into the wilderness with us?"

"Pack it in, pack it out!" said Anna.

Alison gave Anna the thumbs-up sign. "Right!" she said with a grin. From the corner of her eye, she watched Jackie pick up her trash and stuff it in her pocket.

When Alison had bandaged Kate's blister, she stood up and said, "Okay, campers! Check around and make sure you haven't left anything. It's time to get this show on the road!"

Chapter Five

THE WATER IS WIDE

he roar of water rushing over rocks and boulders grew louder and louder, drowning out the calls of the birds. The five hikers soon reached the stream.

"Okay, kids," said Alison. "I can see right now that the water isn't very deep, but it *is* moving pretty swiftly, so we have to be careful in crossing. I'll go first and show you how to cross. If you step on the same rocks I do, you shouldn't have any problem getting to the other side."

Her words were punctuated by the sound of rolling

thunder. "I guess that means we'd better move on," said Alison, trying to sound calm.

"Why can't we cross over there?" asked Kate, pointing upstream. "It's much narrower."

"The water's usually deeper where the stream is narrow," Anna said. "If we fell in, we could get in real trouble."

"Anna's right," said Alison. "The water is probably the shallowest here at the widest part."

"But we'd only have to step on a couple of rocks up there," said Kate. "If we cross here, we have to step on zillions of rocks before we get all the way across."

"I'd rather cross at the narrow part," said Jackie.

"Me, too," said Kate.

Anna shrugged. "It's okay with me," she said. "I guess I'd rather cross the skinny part of the stream. Maybe I'm not as likely to fall in."

Alison threw up her hands. "Okay, okay, you girls win." She laughed, glad they were thinking about something besides the storm.

The hikers walked upstream and Alison pointed out the best flat rocks to use, making certain each girl knew exactly where to step.

"Jackie, Kim. Roll the legs of your pants up as high as you can. Everybody take off your shoes, stuff your socks inside, tie the laces together securely, and hang them around your necks. . . . Ready?"

A bright flash of lightning lit the afternoon sky, soon followed by a huge clap of thunder that rolled in deep waves over the mountaintops. The storm was practically on top of them.

"I hate lightning," Kimberly said in a quivering voice.

"I know, honey," Alison said, putting her arm around Kimberly's shoulder. "But there's nothing I can do about it right now. The best thing we can do is cross this stream as fast and as safely as we can."

Alison thought for a moment. Maybe she could make the crossing into a game for the girls. She turned to the huddled group and took a small bow. Then she stepped back and made her announcement as if she were the ringmaster in a circus.

"And now, ladies and . . . and . . . ladies," she called

out, "for the main attraction of the afternoon you will see Alison the Incredible cross the stream without getting one drop of water on her body. Then, following in her famous footsteps, Kimberly, Jackie, Kate, and Anna will accomplish the same death-defying feat!" She paused, checking to see that everyone had picked up their belongings. "Are you ready?"

"Ready!" the girls cried.

Alison walked to the water's edge. "Here I go!" She stepped out onto a large, flat rock.

"One! Two! Three!" the girls counted her steps as she went from rock to rock.

As she reached the fourth one, Alison turned to look at the group. "See how Alison the Incredible checks ahead to make sure she can—" Alison's foot slipped.

She put her arms out to try to steady herself, but the weight of her backpack pulled her off balance.

Splash!

"Yikes!" she cried out, her left leg plunging into the icy water . "Yeow!" she cried again as the breathtaking cold bit into her.

Bam! A clap of thunder cracked overhead.

The girls scurried to the water's edge. "Are you all right? Did you hurt yourself?"

"I'm okay," Alison said. "The only thing that got wet

was my leg." And my pride, she added to herself.

Pulling her foot out of the water before it turned totally numb, Alison stepped onto the next rock, then onto the bank of the stream, turning immediately to face the girls and let them know she was all right.

Alison smiled brightly, threw her hands into the air and cried, "Ta-da!" She bowed slightly and then called out, "There you see it, ladies and ladies! Alison McCann has just performed her brilliant demonstration of how *not* to cross the stream!"

Kimberly and Kate giggled, then Anna began to clap. "Yea!" she cried. "Yea! Hooray!" The campers cheered.

Alison looked at them solemnly, then bowed. "Thank you! Thank you!" She paused and then said, "And now, Jackie the Magnificent will demonstrate the right way to cross the stream. Then Kate the Great will do her job, followed by Kimberly the Brave and Anna the Fabulous."

She coaxed the girls across one by one: Jackie, then Kate, then Kimberly.

Just as Anna stepped onto the middle rock, a blinding flash of lightning arced overhead. It was followed immediately by a gigantic clap of thunder.

"AAhhh!" came Anna's startled cry. She started to wobble dangerously.

"Anna!" Alison leaped back onto a boulder to

give Anna a hand. But before she could reach her, the little girl slipped sideways and fell. The icy water was up to her waist, soaking her shorts and the bottom of her backpack.

Shock and terror spread over her face. "Help me. I can't swim!"

Reaching down, Alison grabbed Anna's hand and pulled her onto dry land.

She stood shaking and shivering and her teeth chattered as Alison hugged her. "It's okay, Anna. It's going to be all right."

"C-c-c-cold . . . I'm c-c-cold."

"I know, I know. The first thing we have to do is get your wet clothes off."

"But I d-d-don't have d-d-dry clothes. All the s-stuff in my backp-p-pack is wet."

Alison gave her a brave smile. "At least your shoes are still dry. And I have some extra clothes you can wear." She reached into her backpack and pulled out shorts and a pair of socks. "Ta-da!" she said softly, holding up the dry clothes for all the kids to see. "They'll be too big on you, but at least they're dry."

Shaking, Anna said. "Th-thanks. But my shirt is soaking wet, too."

"No problem at all. I'm kind of hot, anyway. Take off

your shirt and you can put on my jacket. You'll be toasty warm. I promise."

Anna nodded.

As she helped Anna change clothes, Alison looked at the other girls. "Are you alright?"

Crash! More thunder rolled across the mountainside.

Kimberly flinched and Alison reached out and squeezed her shoulder.

"Let's get our stuff together and move out of here!" Alison said. Without her jacket the chill wind bit into her arms. That storm's a big one, she thought.

"Okay, Anna, why don't you lead this time? The trail is clear and level ahead. If you jog you'll warm up sooner." In single file, Alison bringing up the rear, the girls trotted through the tall pines.

A few minutes later, Anna cried, "Whoa!" The hikers stopped. "Look!" she cried, her eyes wide.

Chapter Six

THE BEAR FACTS

veryone followed Anna's pointing finger. About fifty feet away, just before the path curved, sat a bear cub. Covered with black fuzzy fur, it was no bigger than a large teddy bear. With its round button eyes, a nose that looked like it was made of shiny leather, and big clumsy paws, it looked like a cuddly stuffed animal.

"Ooo," cried the girls. "He's darling!"

"That's the cutest thing I've ever seen!" said Anna.

Alison just stood and stared. Anna was right. The cub

was cuter than Matilda's kittens, even. Cuter than Duke when he was a puppy.

"Can we pet it?" asked Kimberly.

Reaching over to take Alison's hand, Kate said, "Can we touch him?"

"No," Alison said firmly, trying to sort out what would be the best plan of action. The cub pawed at something in the air but kept its eyes on the hikers.

"Oh, please!" said Jackie.

"No, you can't." Alison kept her voice firm but casual. "When there's a cub around, the mother bear probably isn't very far away." She glanced at the kids, then turned her attention back to where the bear sat staring at them. "I want all of you to do exactly what I tell you." Alison swallowed, wishing she felt as calm as she sounded. "So what we need to do now," she continued in a steady, reassuring voice, "is move slowly away so the mama bear won't get upset. Do you understand?"

The other girls nodded gravely.

Alison placed herself between the cub and the campers. "The smartest thing we can do is just go quietly back down the trail. Is everybody ready?"

"I guess so," said Kate.

"Sure," said Anna.

Even though Alison tried to appear calm, the urgency in her voice was clear. Silence fell over the group as they began to back down the trail. "You kids are doing great . . . really great." She looked toward the cub once more. Its nose began twitching.

Then, to Alison's shock, it started after the girls.

"It's coming for us!" cried Anna, her voice quivering.

"It's leading the mama bear to us so she can eat us for supper!" Jackie shouted.

"Take it easy, kids," said Alison. "Just stay cool. Everything's going to be all right." Alison's pulse beat like a giant pump in her ears. The granola bars! Alison remembered all the funny stories she'd heard about bears eating hikers' food. The cub must smell them in my backpack. "You girls keep on going," she said. "I'll follow you in just a minute."

Slipping her pack from her shoulders as she continued to back up, Alison reached inside and grabbed a granola bar. Then she pulled it out, unwrapped it and tossed it as far away from her as she could.

Sniffing, the cub scrambled over to the bar and picked it up between its paws.

He took the bait! Alison thought happily. But she

celebrated too soon. At that very moment, a large black bear appeared out of the bushes near the cub.

"The mama!" the girls cried. "Help!"

As if they all thought as one, the girls turned from the trail.

"No!" cried Alison. "Don't run!"

But it was too late. The four terrified campers scattered in every direction.

Alison watched as the mother bear ambled over to her cub, then sniffed the granola bar that the small bear still held between its paws. She opened her mouth and took a bite, then stood beside her cub as it ate the rest. Afterwards, mother and child waddled off into the woods as if they hadn't a care in the world.

Satisfied that the danger had passed, Alison turned to look for her campers. But there wasn't one ponytail, one backpack, not even one granola wrapper to be found. All four of her charges had disappeared into the woods.

Shivering, Alison stood for a moment and listened. But all she heard was the wild, lonely sound of the wind whooshing through the branches of the pines. What am I going to do? she thought. I'm responsible for those girls. What could I have been thinking of? I should have listened to Becky. She told me to stick to the path marked on the map. If I'd done that, if we'd looked for the clues and followed them, we wouldn't have run into the bears. And, she thought guiltily, if I'd followed directions, maybe crossing the stream would have been easier and Anna wouldn't have fallen in.

Alison cupped her hands around her mouth. "Hey, all you Sierra campers out there! Come on back to the path!" she called. "The bears are gone! Everything's all right. You can come back now!"

Silence.

"Come on now!" Alison called out again. "Campers! You can come out now!"

"Over here!" a tiny voice called out from a distance.

"I'm over here!" echoed another.

Alison stood in the middle of the path. "I'm going to start talking," she said in as loud a voice as she could manage without screaming. "All you have to do is listen and follow the sound of my voice." She paused and waited for an answer. "Hey, out there, are you following the sound?"

"I am!" said a voice. Scratched and bedraggled, Jackie stepped out from behind a tree. "Are the bears really gone?" she asked.

"Jackie!" Alison cried with a wide smile. "See, girls, Jackie's here and she's safe and the bears are all gone so you can come on out! Just listen to my voice and walk toward it."

"I'm over here," said Kate, peeking around a bush.

Alison smiled. "Hooray! Kate's here, too!"

Crash! Lightning flashed nearby and loud thunder broke overhead.

Scared out of hiding by the roar of the thunder, Anna ran into the clearing. Then Alison called out again for Kimberly, but she was still nowhere to be found.

Alison looked at the three girls who stood trembling beside her. Their hands and faces were smudged. Jackie had dirt all over the side of her jeans leg and Anna's curls were tangled with twigs and leaves.

"I know you're all still scared," Alison said. "But is anybody really hurt?"

The girls looked at each other. Anna held out her arm to show Alison the deep scratch near her elbow.

"I cut my leg," Jackie said, "but I don't think it's very bad."

"Okay," said Alison. "I think both of those things can wait a couple of minutes. I'll help you as soon as we find Kimberly."

Too scared and exhausted to speak, the girls just nodded slowly.

"Now listen to me," said Alison. "This is important. Very important. Do not leave my side for any reason at all. Do you understand?"

"Yes," croaked Kate.

"Yes," whispered the others.

"When I start walking around I want you to stick with me like you're my shadow. Understand?"

The girls nodded.

"Okay, then, here we go!" Alison cupped her hands over her mouth and called out, "Kimberly! Hey, Kimberly! Can you hear me? It's Alison. Come on now, Kimberly. Everything's okay! I promise."

"The bears ran away!" yelled Kate.

"We're all safe!" Jackie called. "You can come out now!"

More thunder and lightning cracked overhead. The sky had disappeared behind rolling banks of clouds.

Where could Kimberly have gone? She was so sweet and shy. And so scared of storms. Alison pictured her huddling under a bush somewhere, shivering, maybe crying, her hands over her ears and her eyes shut tight. She headed slowly into the trees. The three campers followed close at her heels.

"Come on, Kimberly!" Alison called out. Her throat had turned dry and her voice was growing hoarse. "It's okay now, Kimberly! Just follow the sound of my voice and

you'll be back in no time!"

"I'm here," a tiny voice squeaked. "Over here!"

"Kimberly!" Alison cried.

"Kimberly!" the little campers squealed.

In one step, Alison folded the frightened child in the safety of her arms. She thought she felt a raindrop on her head, but she wasn't sure.

Chapter
Seven

LOST IN THE WOODS

lison spent the next few minutes helping the girls calm down and clean up their cuts and scratches with tissues and fresh water from her water bottle.

Anna had a deep scratch on her arm, and after washing that as best as she could, Alison covered it with one of the bandages she carried in her backpack. The cut on Jackie's leg required a bigger dressing, so she took one of her own clean socks, used her pocket knife to cut part of it into a long strip and tied the sock around Jackie's leg. After tending each girl, Alison gave her a big hug.

She felt chilled, tired and worried. In the last few minutes, the clouds had turned black. The wind had picked up, bringing with it gusts of cold mountain air. Her bare arms prickled with goose bumps as she stood up. What will I do if we're caught in the storm? she asked herself. How will I keep them all warm and dry?

"Are we far from the campsite?" Anna asked.

Alison looked at the girls. "I'm not sure. But I don't think we're *that* far away."

"Why don't you check your map?" suggested Jackie.

Alison was embarrassed. "I—I hate to tell you this, but . . . I lost it," she said. For a moment, nobody said anything. Four pairs of eyes stared at Alison in disappointment and disbelief.

Then Kate took a deep breath and said, "But you didn't tell us the truth."

"I know," said Alison. "I guess it fell out of my pocket earlier. I didn't tell you because I was afraid you'd get worried."

"But you didn't tell the *truth*," Anna protested.

"I'm sorry," Alison said. "I really am."

"Does that mean we're lost?" she asked.

Alison sighed. "Well," she said, "it means we're going to have to use all our wits to find the way. The one thing I remember from the map is that after the shortcut our official trail crosses the stream and curves south toward the campsite."

Alison squatted on her heels and cleared away the leaves and pine needles in front of her. "Look. This way is north, and this is the stream." As she spoke, she drew an arrow and then a squiggly line in the dirt. "The shortcut crosses the stream here—" she made an X "—and

eventually goes
southeast to the
campsite. When
you ran from the
bears, we got off the shortcut trail,
and now I'm not sure which direction to go in."

"It's too dark to tell where the sun is." Kimberly's voice was very quiet.

"That doesn't sound very good," said Anna.

"Maybe the clouds will break soon." Alison tried to sound strong and confident. "Anyhow, all we need to do is find the stream again and go southeast. Now—"

"I hear—" Kate began.

"Hush, Kate. Please don't interrupt now."

"But—" Kate protested.

"Please. This is important."

Almost ready to cry, Kate looked at Alison with a stubborn expression. "You don't understand," she insisted. "The stream is over there!"

Startled, Alison looked at Kate and asked, "How do you know that?"

Kate shook her head. "That's not just the sound of the wind blowing in the trees," she said. "If you listen, you can hear water, too."

Alison listened silently for a moment, then shook her head at herself. "You're right, Kate. I guess I should slow down and listen," she replied a bit sheepishly.

The girls smiled, but still waited for Alison to tell them what to do.

"Now that we know to face away from the stream," Alison continued, "if we just head southeast, we should eventually run into all the other campers. The tent site isn't very far at all." She wiped a few raindrops off her chilly arms. Even if we get wet, she thought, the girls will feel more self-confident if they help find the way.

"Kate," she said cheerfully, "can you figure out which way is southeast?"

"I've heard moss grows on the north side of the trees," said Kate, "so we could find some moss."

"Well, that's sort of true." Alison paused, then nodded encouragingly. "Actually, it's a pretty good idea, Kate. More than half the time, moss *does* grow on the north side. But where south winds blow cold, it will grow on the south side."

She looked at the other girls. "Any other ideas?"

"If it were night, I could show you where the North Star is by following the Big Dipper," said Anna.

"That's good. But since it's not night . . . and since we don't know where moss grows in these parts of the mountains . . ." Alison coached.

The girls looked at each other and shrugged.

Alison smiled. "I'll show you a special trick," she said, "for figuring out your direction. It's not as accurate as a compass, but it works pretty well." She picked up a short twig and unbuckled her watch, then stepped into a small clearing where the light was still just bright enough to create shadows.

She held her watch in front of the hikers. "You point the hour hand of the watch toward the light. We can't see the sun

because it's cloudy and we're surrounded by trees. So to find your direction, use any kind of straight stick to make sure the shadow it casts cuts straight across the hour number to the center of the watch. Now," she continued dramatically, "imagine where the middle point is between the hour hand and twelve noon. And that direction is south."

"Wow!" said Kimberly. "That's really cool!"

"It sure is!" said Kate.

"So which way is southeast?" Alison asked.

"That way!" said Anna, pointing to the left side of south.

Alison reached over and tousled Anna's curls. "And just how did you know that?"

Anna leaned down and pointed to the map that Alison had scratched into the dirt. "Because if you're facing south, west is always to the right of south and east is to the left."

"Bravo!" cried Alison.

"How do we find our way back to camp?" asked Jackie, as large drops of rain made craters on the dirt map.

Chapter
Eight

OUT OF DANGER

o what do you think?" Alison said as they began
walking. "Is it time for a song?"

The girls nodded.

"Row, row, row your boat . . ." Kimberly sang shyly.

Alison smiled, urging the girls to continue singing,
then she took up the second part, making it a round.

They marched down the trail singing loudly.

"I'm tired," said Jackie.

"*Really* tired," Anna chimed in.

"Me, too," said Kate.

"We all are," said Alison. "But hang in there. We can't be very far from camp now."

With that, a huge clap of thunder crashed overhead. The rain fell harder and faster.

Alison glanced up at the sky, then at her weary-looking campers.

Suddenly, Kate's hand shot up. "I know!" she said. "Let's play 'Simon Says!'"

"That's a baby game," Jackie frowned.

"Who cares if it's babyish," said Anna. "It's still fun."

"You be Simon, Kate," said Kimberly.

"Way to go!" said Alison. "Okay, Sierras, let's move!"

The rain fell in heavy sheets as "Simon" scurried down the trail.

Fifteen minutes later, the exhausted, soaked campers and their Junior Counselor hopped into camp on their left feet, quacking like ducks.

"Look!" cried Janet Higgens, poking her head out of a tent. "It's the lost Sierras!"

Cheering campers and worried counselors ran out to hug the girls, and quickly pulled them inside a huge tent. When the others heard that the Sierra kids had actually seen two bears, the girls became instant celebrities.

As the girls toweled themselves off, Janet said, "You

still lose the prize, Kate. We Tetons got here first. You're going to have to make all the Tetons' beds the morning after we get back to camp."

Discouraged, Kate looked at the ground. "Alison said that was just a rumor, that there wasn't really a prize for getting here first."

"Well, you thought you'd have to do it, so you should," said Janet.

"Hold on a minute!" said Alison, raising her hand. "If anybody gets their beds made around here, it's the Sierra campers. *They're* the ones who deserve it. And I'm the one who's going to enjoy making each and every bed the morning after we return to our cabin."

It wasn't until bedtime that Alison remembered where she'd be two days later.

In the morning, Alison sat down outside the tent with Anna, Kate, Jackie, and Kimberly. The crisp, clean air was scented with pine. Birds chattered in the branches

of the trees and a hawk soared overhead searching for breakfast. The storm had passed and the sun shone brightly through the trees, casting long morning shadows across the forest floor.

"I just want to tell you how sorry I am about yesterday," Alison said. "I was in charge and even though I expected you to follow the rules, I didn't follow them myself. I'm really proud of all of you. You Sierras really pulled together and showed what teamwork can do."

After giving each girl a big hug, Alison went for a

walk. She found a comfortable seat on a log next to the stream and sat quietly for a few minutes. Staring into the swift, rushing water, she thought about all that had happened to her. Finally, she reached into her backpack and pulled out a small mirror. It's time to go back, Alison thought. Looking at her face in the shiny surface, she smiled.

The next day Alison joined Keisha, Megan, and Heather at their usual corner.

"Hey, Ali!" Keisha called as she came up. "Ellie told us you went to the attic yesterday. Was it fun?"

"I'm not sure fun is the right word," Alison said laughing, "but it was definitely an adventure I won't ever forget."

"Why? What happened?" asked Heather. She took the last bite of her breakfast apple and tossed the core into a trash can.

Alison thought for a moment. "I'll tell you the whole story at lunch, okay? Right now I want to say how sorry I am for the way I acted in Science. I—"

"You don't have to apologize again," said Heather. "We're best friends."

"Everybody makes mistakes, Ali," said Keisha. "It was no big deal. Right, Megan?"

Alison, Heather, and Keisha turned to their friend.

Megan looked thoughtful and serious. "It's okay, Ali. It didn't hurt very much at all." Megan's green eyes began to twinkle, and the corners of her mouth turned up. She laughed as she put her arm around Alison's shoulder. "I was just really *shocked*, if you know what I mean."

Alison giggled. "I sure do," she said.

Diary

Dear Diary,

   If you were a person, I'd tell you to sit down.

Because you're not going to believe this. You know

I don't normally tell you about grades. But this is

different. I got a 100% on my spelling test today!

Megan studied with me yesterday afternoon and

then she quizzed me all the way to school this

morning. It worked!

   School's better in other ways, too. We're

studying rocks and minerals in Science class now. I

love to look at geodes. Every time you open one,

it's a surprise. Ms. Joseph even showed us one

that had fifty-million-year-old water inside! You

could actually see the water through the crystal.

She also showed us a piece of amber with a bug

stuck inside. She brought lots of other gems and

minerals to class, too. Did you know there are

diamonds in the United States? You can actually go diamond hunting in Arkansas! Someday I'm going to do that.

Good news! My father's taking my three brothers on a camping trip this weekend He asked if I wanted to go along but I figured I'd had enough experience with nature to last me for a little while. I have a lot to think about, anyway.

Actually, staying home isn't such a bad deal. I can't wait to have Mom and the house all to myself. My brothers really get to me sometimes. There are days when I feel like I'm living with aliens under my own roof. I can't figure out how they got so weird.

In honor of this special boy-free weekend, the Magic Attic Club is having a sleep-over at my house tomorrow night. I think I'm awfully lucky to have such great friends. In the afternoon, we're going to bake chocolate chip cookies, everybody's favorite. Then after dinner, we're going to watch The Wizard of Oz.

On Saturday, Mom said she'd take us to the Museum of Science and Industry. I can't wait. I hear they've got lots of new exhibits, including a virtual reality trip to Mars and a human maze. If you reach the goal at the center of the maze in less than ten minutes, you get a prize. Even though I love to compete, this time someone else can be the leader.

I'm out of news for now.

Love, Me

Alison

JOIN THE MAGIC ATTIC CLUB!

You can enjoy every adventure of the Magic Attic Club just by reading all the books. And there's more!

You can have a whole world of fun with the dolls, outfits, and accessories that are based on the books. And since Alison, Keisha, Heather, and Megan can wear one another's clothes, you can relive their adventures, or create new ones of your own!

To join the Magic Attic Club, just fill out this postcard and drop it in the mail, or call toll free **1-800-221-6972**. We'll send you a **free** membership kit

including a poster, bookmark, postcards, and a catalog with all four dolls.

With your first purchase of a doll, you'll also receive your own key to the attic. And it's FREE!

Yes, I want to join the Magic Attic Club!

My name is _____

My address is _____

City _____ State _____ Zip _____

Birth date _____ Parent's Signature _____

11915

And send a catalog to my friend, too!

My friend's name is _____

Address _____

City _____ State _____ Zip _____

11916

If someone has already used the postcard from this book and you would like a free Magic Attic Club catalog, just send your full name and address to:

Magic Attic Club
866 Spring Street
P.O. Box 9712
Portland, ME 04104-9954

Or call toll free
1-800-775-9272

Code: 11917